LEAD THE WAY,
VELOCIRAPTOR!

based on text by Dawn Bentley
Illustrated by Karen Carr

Little®
Soundprints

For Nile Alexander. Love, Aunt Dawn. — D.B.

Dedicated with love and appreciation to Dr. Bonnie F. Jacobs of the Environmental Science Program at SMU, whose work educates and enlightens. — K.C.

Published by Soundprints Division of Trudy Corporation, Norwalk, Connecticut.

Book design: Marcin Pilchowski
Editor: Laura Gates Galvin
Editorial assistance: Brian E. Giblin

First Edition 2004
10 9 8 7 6 5 4 3 2 1
Printed in China

Acknowledgements:
        Our very special thanks to Dr. Brett-Surman of the Smithsonian Institution's National Museum of Natural History.
        Soundprints would also like to thank Ellen Nanney and Katie Mann of the Smithsonian Institution for their help in the creation of this book.

LEAD THE WAY,
VELOCIRAPTOR!

based on text by Dawn Bentley
Illustrated by Karen Carr

SMITHSONIAN INSTITUTION

A note to the reader:

Throughout this story you will see words in **bold letters**. There is more information about these words in the glossary. The glossary is in the back of the book.

The land is hot and dry. A Velociraptor looks down at the valley below.

Velociraptor jumps to the top of a **ridge**. He is small, but he is smart and fast!

Velociraptor sees others from his **pack**. He joins them. They will look for food together.

Velociraptor runs as fast as he can. He is one of the fastest runners in the land!

Velociraptor sees a **Gallimimus**. The Gallimimus is very big. But Velociraptor is very smart. He can catch the Gallimimus.

The Velociraptor pack circles the big dinosaur. The Gallimimus can't fight them off.

The Velociraptor pack sees an **Oviraptor** eating some eggs. The Oviraptor quickly runs away. The Velociraptor pack eats all of the eggs.

A **Protoceratops** and an Oviraptor are fighting. When they see the Velociraptor, they run away. No one wants to fight the Velociraptor!

Velociraptor lies down to rest. He cleans his claws. He takes good care of them.

A little mammal runs by. Velociraptor traps it. Velociraptor is a good hunter!

Velociraptor hears something. He and the pack leap to their feet. They are always ready for action!

Glossary

Ridge: A long narrow hilltop or range of hills or mountains.

Pack: A large number of animals that live and hunt together.

Gallimimus: A fast-running dinosaur with very long legs, a long neck, and a long beak.

Oviraptor: A dinosaur with long, slender legs and huge hands with three long and slender fingers.

Protoceratops: These horned dinosaurs were the first dinosaurs known through every stage of life.

ABOUT THE *VELOCIRAPTOR*
(vel-OS-i-RAP-tor)

Velociraptor lived about 75 million years ago. It weighed up to 50 pounds and was just three feet tall. That's probably smaller than you are.

Velociraptor was small compared to the bigger dinosaurs that lived during that time. But *Velociraptor* had a big brain and was very smart, which made it a great hunter.

Velociraptor could run up to 25 miles per hour and change direction quickly by swinging its tail. That means it was probably able to catch almost any dinosaur it chased.

Other dinosaurs that lived with Velociraptor:

Gallimimus (GAL-i-MIEM-us)

Oviraptor (OH-vi-RAP-tor)

Protoceratops (PROH-toe-SER-a-tops)

Tenontosaurus (te-NON-toe-SAWR-us)